D0364211

I remember the monsters that lurked in and around my bedroom when I was very young. I was sure they were there! Somehow I managed to survive and never gave them much thought until later in life when I was sitting with my guru and dear teacher, Ma Jaya Sati Bhagavati. As part of her teachings, adults were taught how to deal with lurking monsters – real or imagined. Now some years after her passing, I've incorporated those teachings into a book for children.

When I first wrote the story in the form of a poem, I shared the words with family and a few friends, as writers will do. Upon hearing the story and told I wanted to have illustrations, my friend, Marti Ladd, strongly suggested that the story be of my father and myself. That turned out to be a really good idea! So I sent the words to Kathy Garren and asked her to illustrate the poem with drawings of me and my dad.

Kathy has always been really good at drawing pictures of me that I actually like. Even so, I was wonderfully surprised to see how well the story came to life, using old photos and newspaper clippings to create the illustrations with some degree of plausibility.

So now my fifth book for children is finished and going to print, but before I start moving on to the next unknown adventure, I want to say 'Thank You' to everyone who helped bring this book to life.

My daughter, Annie, for another flurry of activity, Cindy for putting it all together, Kathy for the back and forth required to make it perfect, Marti who insisted on keeping it personal, and most especially to Ma for the wisdom and knowledge concerning "MONSTERS."

— Arlo Guthrie

First Edition

Library of Congress Control Number: 2015953636

Guthrie, Arlo

Summary: A kid, with help from his dad, confronts the monsters in his room.

ISBN: 978-0-9961358-2-5

Manufactured By Quality Printing, Co. in Pittsfield, MA, September 2015

Rising Son International, Ltd.
Washington, MA

MONSTERS

BY ARLO GUTHRIE

ILLUSTRATED BY KATHY GARREN

RISING SON INTERNATIONAL, LTD.

It doesn't take long to know I'm not alone

There's all kind of monsters invading my home

There's more in the closet and in the old chest

But it's under my bed where they like it the best

I pull up the covers and curl into a ball

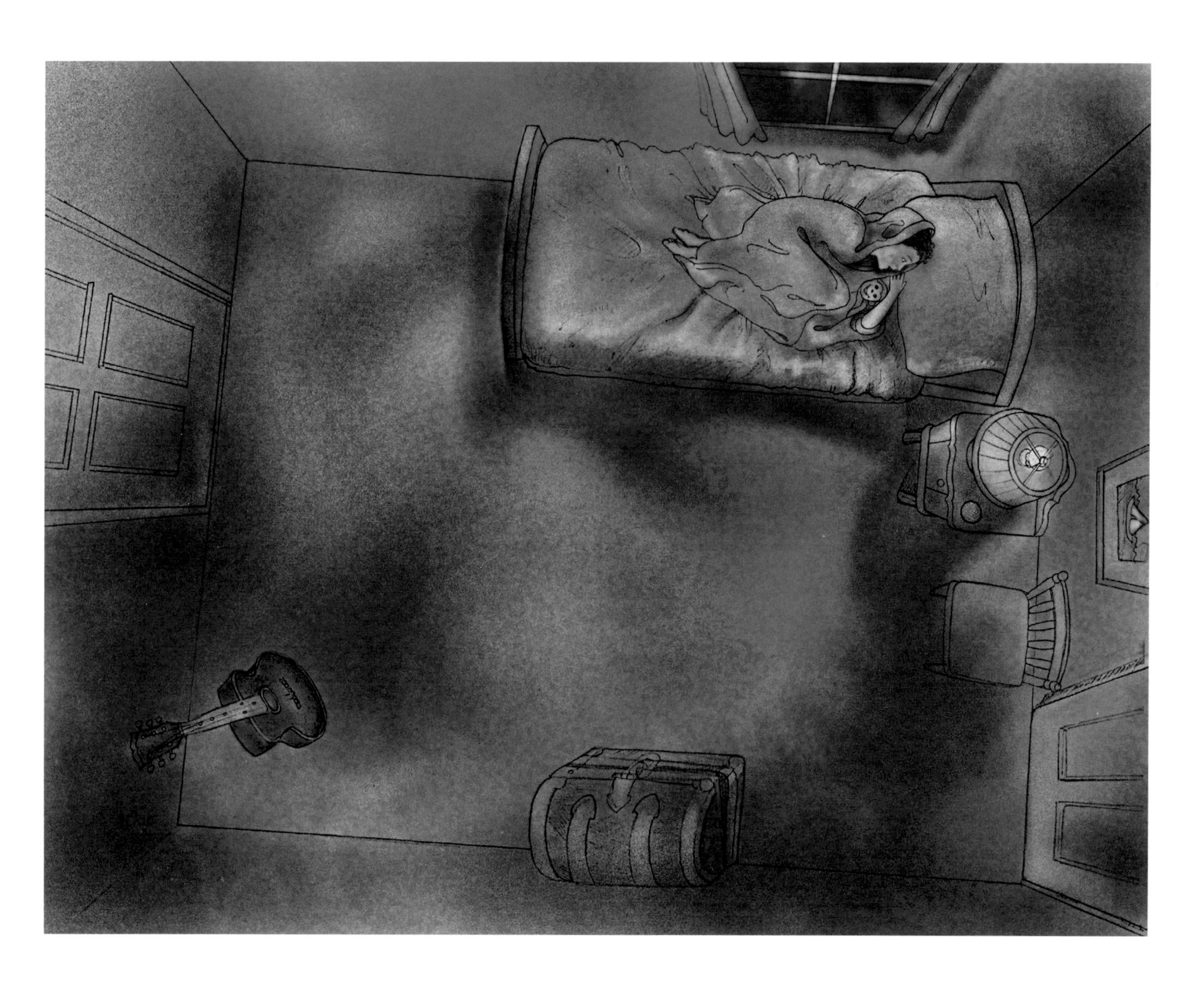

I don't want my hands or my poor feet to fall

Over the edges where monsters can munch

It's nighttime for me, but for them I'm just lunch

There's yellow and green ones, there's purple and blue

Monsters in colors of *every* known hue

Sometimes there's just one,
and at other times herds

I cannot describe them in everyday words

When my father comes into my room
through the door

I turn on the light and I point to the floor

“There’s monsters,” I whisper.
“They’re big and they’re mean.

They're snarly and filthy,
though some are quite clean."

"Of course there are monsters,"
my father's voice said

"But they're not in the room,
they are just in your head."

“When a monster comes near,
point your finger and say

‘Who are you, you monster?’ And don’t look away.”

“For monsters can only appear when you’re scared

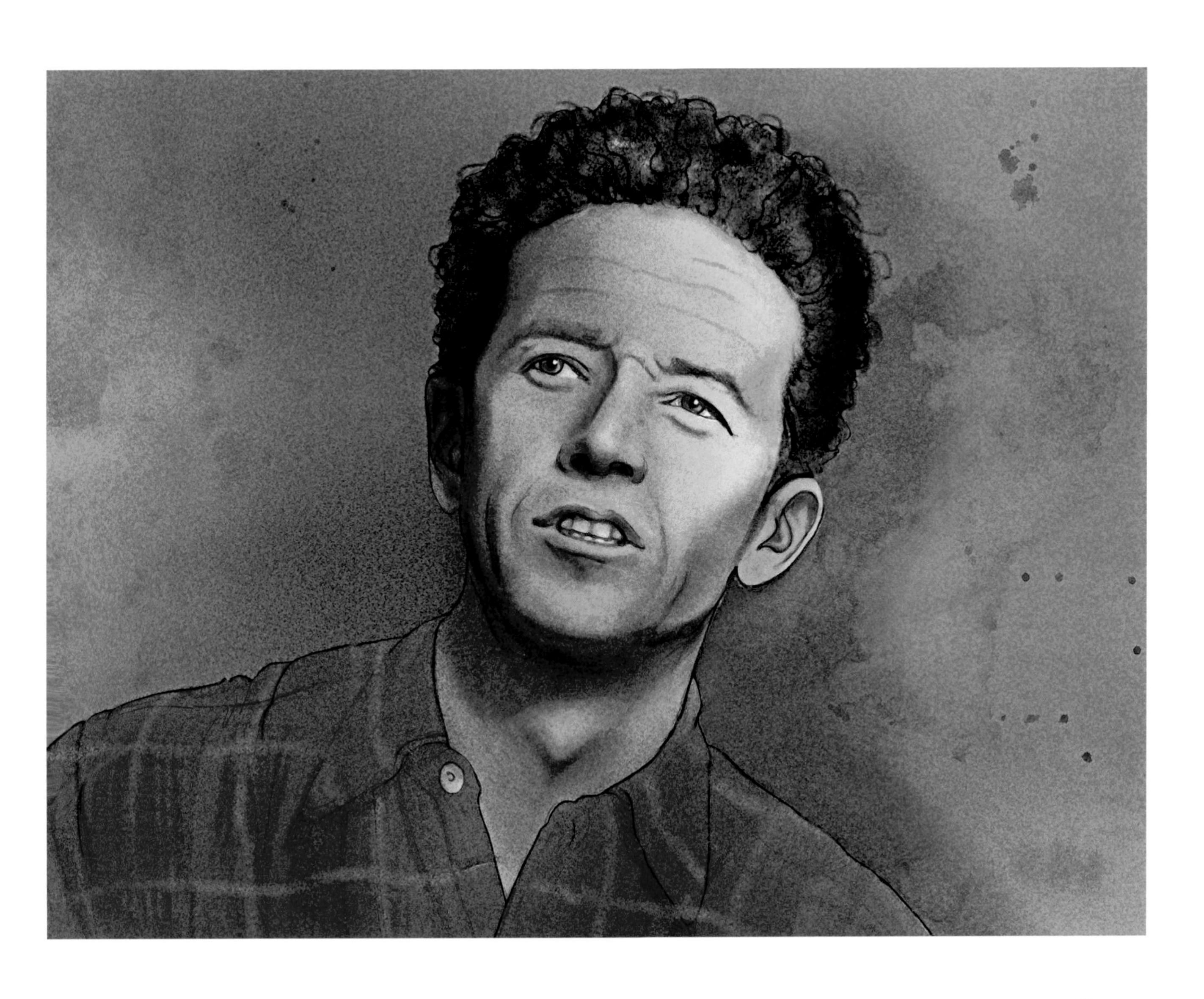

But if you have courage then you'll be prepared."

"The monsters will leave when you turn out the light."

So to all of you monsters, *goodbye* and *goodnight.*